D1742925

CLOTHING
INSPIRED BY NATURE

by Wendy Hinote Lanier

FOCUS READERS

WWW.FOCUSREADERS.COM

Copyright © 2019 by Focus Readers, Lake Elmo, MN 55042. All rights reserved. No part of this book may be reproduced or utilized in any form or by any means without written permission from the publisher.

Focus Readers is distributed by North Star Editions:
sales@northstareditions.com | 888-417-0195

Produced for Focus Readers by Red Line Editorial.

Content Consultant: Veronika Kapsali, Reader Material Technology and Design, London College of Fashion

Photographs ©: Bernd Thissen/picture-alliance/dpa/AP Images, cover, 1; urbans/ Shutterstock Images, 4–5; Marian Cernansky/Shutterstock Images, 7; © Kraig Biocraft Laboratories, 8; michelangeloop/iStockphoto, 10–11; Anton_Ivanov/Shutterstock Images, 12; Johnny Hanson/Houston Chronicle/AP Images, 15; Clouds Hill Imaging Ltd./Corbis Documentary/Getty Images, 17; gerenme/iStockphoto, 18–19; Red Line Editorial, 21; Jill McIntire/Shutterstock Images, 23; adisa/iStockphoto, 24–25; Bildagentur Zoonar GmbH/ Shutterstock Images, 27; AleksandarDickov/iStockphoto, 29

ISBN
978-1-63517-939-2 (hardcover)
978-1-64185-041-4 (paperback)
978-1-64185-243-2 (ebook pdf)
978-1-64185-142-8 (hosted ebook)

Library of Congress Control Number: 2018932005

Printed in the United States of America
Mankato, MN
May, 2018

ABOUT THE AUTHOR

Wendy Hinote Lanier is a native Texan and former elementary teacher who writes and speaks for children and adults on a variety of topics. She is the author of more than 30 books for children and young adults.

TABLE OF CONTENTS

CHAPTER 1

PROTECTIVE CLOTHING

Clothing does more than make people look good. Humans need clothing to protect their bodies. Some of today's clothing protects people in dangerous situations. **High-tech** designs make this type of clothing possible. Many scientists find ideas for these designs in nature. The scientists identify a problem.

Firefighters wear flame-resistant clothing to prevent burns.

Then they study how plants or animals solve it. They make inventions that copy these solutions. This process is called biomimicry.

Biomimicry is responsible for some of the newest protective clothing. For example, police officers and soldiers use body armor to stay safe. But most armor is tough and inflexible. Researchers turned to spider silk to solve this problem. Spider silk is one of the strongest fibers in nature. One company is using spider silk to make a new kind of body armor.

Unfortunately, it can be difficult to produce large amounts of spider silk. Spiders do not work well in groups. So,

Spider silk can be stretched several times its length without breaking.

researchers decided to put spider **DNA** into silk worms. The silk worms then make large amounts of silk fibers. These fibers are similar to spider silk. Using the silk fibers, researchers created a strong cloth known as Dragon Silk. This material can be used to make protective clothing.

This silk worm has been filled with spider DNA. It is ready to produce spider silk.

In 2016, the US Army hired the creators of Dragon Silk. The Army wanted them to design body armor for soldiers.

Nature is also inspiring new kinds of flame-resistant materials. For example, researchers have developed a new coating for cloth. It is a mixture of clay, fish DNA, and a substance found in lobster shells. The coating is applied in layers. It keeps clothing safe from fire. And it is even **eco-friendly**.

A STICKY IDEA

A famous example of biomimicry is Velcro. In 1948, a Swiss inventor returned from a hike with seed burrs stuck to his clothes. When he looked closely, he saw the burrs had tiny hooks. The hooks had caught on the loops in his clothes. He made two kinds of cloth inspired by the burrs. One cloth had hooks. The other had loops. The two fabrics attached together firmly. It took eight years to perfect the design.

CHAPTER 2

STAYING WARM AND DRY

Clothing can protect people in extreme weather. One example is a jacket inspired by penguins. Many penguins hunt in freezing water. Their feathers keep them warm. At the bottom of each feather is a muscle. In water, the muscle pulls the feather down so it lies flat. This gives the penguin a smooth, waterproof coat.

Advanced clothing technology allows athletes to train and compete in cold weather.

In Antarctica, penguins swim in waters as cold as 29 degrees Fahrenheit (−2°C).

On land, the muscles relax. When this happens, the feathers form a thick coat filled with air. This protects the penguin against wind.

An **insert** for jackets mimics penguin feathers. The insert is made of two layers of fabric. Strips of fabric connect the two layers. When the strips stand up straight, the jacket fills with air. When the strips lie flat, the jacket becomes thin and tight. The insert protects people in wet, cold, and windy weather.

Even in cold weather, exercise causes people to sweat. The moisture under their clothes can make them feel cold. To solve this problem, researchers are inventing clothing that releases moisture. This new type of fabric was inspired by plants.

Plants give off extra water through a process called transpiration. During transpiration, small openings in leaves release water and oxygen. One clothing company makes outerwear inspired by this process. In cold weather, the fabric's fibers stay closed. This keeps water out.

But when the person's body warms, the fibers open. Heat and sweat can escape.

Another type of outerwear is inspired by the lotus plant. Lotus leaves are covered with tiny bumps and a waxy material. This surface allows water to bead up and roll off. Meanwhile, the water carries away dust and dirt.

A SMART SCARF

In 2011, a designer created a new type of scarf. It was based on a hornbeam leaf. Hornbeam leaves have closed folds. When the leaves pop out of their buds, the folds open. The wool scarf folds into a small package, much like a hornbeam leaf. It can fit inside a pocket or purse. When opened, the scarf creates a large, warm wrap for the neck.

Many companies are using advanced technology to make waterproof clothing.

By studying lotus plants, researchers found a new way of making waterproof clothing. They did this by applying special coatings to fabric. These coatings create a slick surface with tiny bumps. The fabric then mimics the surface of a lotus leaf. It stops water from soaking into the fibers. Instead, the water slides right off.

SHARKSKIN

Sharks are inspiring new technologies in clothing. Sharkskin is made up of flexible layers of small, tooth-like structures. As a shark swims, these "teeth" direct water over the shark's body. This allows for swift, easy movement. It also keeps organisms such as algae from clinging to the shark.

A new clothing product acts similarly to sharkskin. In 2000, Speedo introduced swimwear called Fastskin. Fastskin is a stretchy material with a surface of V-shaped ridges. The ridges were based on the tooth-like structures of sharkskin. The full Fastskin suit first appeared at the 2000 Olympics.

Many Olympians who wore Fastskin suits won medals. It is unclear whether the suits' ridged surface helped lead to their success. Still, Olympic officials decided that Fastskin might

The small structures on sharkskin are called dermal denticles.

work too well. The material was banned from Olympic competition in 2009.

Another shark-inspired product is Sharklet. Sharklet is a material that can be added to surfaces. The material's pattern keeps **bacteria** from clinging to surfaces. It mimics how sharkskin wards off small algae. Sharklet helps prevent the spread of disease-causing germs. The pattern can be applied to cloth and hard surfaces in hospitals. It can also be used in public restrooms.

CHAPTER 3

EARTH-FRIENDLY CLOTHES

Making colorful fabrics is often harmful to the environment. The process uses large amounts of water, energy, and dyes. Most dyes are made using chemicals. Sometimes, these chemicals end up in rivers and streams. They can also harm the people who work with them.

The production of one cotton shirt uses 700 gallons (2,650 L) of water.

The morpho butterfly has inspired a dye-free cloth. Morpho butterflies are bright blue. Their color is the result of tiny, overlapping scales. These scales produce color by bending, absorbing, and reflecting light.

Morphotex is a cloth inspired by the morpho butterfly. This cloth produces color in a similar way. Unlike most clothing, it does not use dye. Instead, the cloth's fibers are arranged in layers. The fibers interact with light, similar to the butterfly's scales.

The thickness of the layers changes the color of the cloth. Morphotex can be red, green, blue, or violet. The idea behind Morphotex has also been used on electronic screens.

Some designers are using natural materials to grow eco-friendly fabric.

CREATING COLOR

Morpho butterfly scales interact with sunlight to produce shades of blue.

One designer was inspired by kombucha. This is a drink made from bacteria, **yeast**, and sweet tea. The bacteria and yeast cause a chemical change in the tea. As a result, a substance called cellulose forms on the drink. The designer uses a similar process to grow large sheets of cellulose.

POLLINATION STATIONS

Bees spread pollen when they land on flowers. This process allows more plants to grow. But in recent years, many bees have been dying. Bee populations are especially low in cities. To help solve this problem, one designer created bee-friendly clothing. She covered cloth with a nectar-like mixture. She also added images of plant pollen. When hung or worn outside, the clothing attracts bees.

A layer of bacterial cellulose forms on the surface of kombucha.

When the sheets dry, they form a leathery material. She uses this material to make dresses, jackets, and even shoes.

Nature inspired another designer to make an eco-friendly coat. The designer tucked seeds into the coat's wool fibers. When winter is over, the coat can be planted. The wool acts as fertilizer. In summer, the seeds grow into food.

CHAPTER 4

DESIGNS OF THE FUTURE

Nature is inspiring scientists to solve challenging problems in new ways. Nature-inspired clothing protects people in the outdoors. It can also benefit the environment. However, creating new products takes time. Many clothing designs are still in the early stages.

Nature will continue to influence protective, outdoor, and everyday clothing.

One possible design features **artificial** muscles. Scientists studied muscles in animals, including octopus legs and elephant trunks. Then they recreated the muscles out of tiny **carbon** tubes. They hope to use the muscles in clothing for older people. Older people often have weak muscles. The new clothing could give them more strength. This would help people stay active as they age.

Scientists are also working on new types of **camouflage**. They are studying squids for inspiration. Squids have color-changing cells just below their skin. When they expand or contract the cells, their color changes. This allows squids

A squid uses its camouflage to catch and eat a fish.

to blend in with their surroundings. Scientists hope to create clothing that works in a similar way. This technology could be especially useful to the military.

Squids have also inspired self-repairing clothing. Squids use suckers to grab their prey. These suckers contain sharp teeth.

Proteins from the teeth are strong and flexible. Scientists are recreating this protein to make cloth that repairs itself. They do this by covering the cloth with a coating of the protein. If the cloth rips, they simply add water. The proteins then spread toward the rip. This reconnects the torn fabric. Scientists hope to use self-repairing cloth in everyday clothing. In the future, a liquid form of the protein might be available. The liquid would help clothes repair while they are washed.

Nature is a source of inspiration for many kinds of technology. And clothing is no exception. Thanks to nature, scientists are changing the world of fashion.

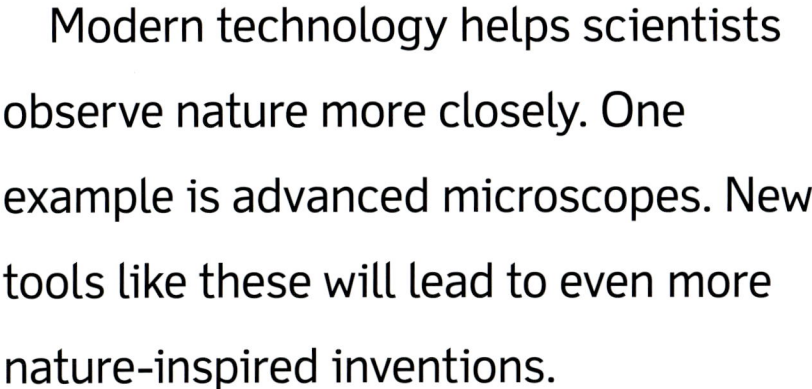

In the future, a liquid form of protein could fix ripped clothes.

Modern technology helps scientists observe nature more closely. One example is advanced microscopes. New tools like these will lead to even more nature-inspired inventions.

FOCUS ON
CLOTHING INSPIRED BY NATURE

Write your answers on a separate piece of paper.

1. Write a sentence describing one of the inventions featured in Chapter 4.

2. Do you think Olympic swimmers should be able to use Fastskin? Why or why not?

3. What is one of the strongest fibers found in nature?
- **A.** cotton
- **B.** Morphotex
- **C.** spider silk

4. How is recycled clothing eco-friendly?
- **A.** It saves Earth's resources by reusing old material.
- **B.** It adds to Earth's resources by fertilizing plants.
- **C.** It encourages pollination by attracting bees.

Answer key on page 32.

GLOSSARY

artificial
Made by humans instead of occurring naturally.

bacteria
Single-celled living things. They can be useful or harmful.

camouflage
A pattern that is designed to look like its surroundings.

carbon
One of the basic chemical elements of all living things.

DNA
The genetic material in the cells of living organisms.

eco-friendly
Not harmful to the environment.

high-tech
Using advanced technology.

insert
An object that is placed inside another object.

proteins
Molecules that are important in telling a living cell what to do.

yeast
A type of fungus used to make bread, alcohol, and other foods and drinks.

TO LEARN MORE

BOOKS

Becker, Helaine. *Zoobots: Wild Robots Inspired by Real Animals*. Toronto: Kids Can Press, 2014.

Gregory, Josh. *From Butterfly Wings to . . . Display Technology*. Ann Arbor, MI: Cherry Lake Publishing, 2014.

Mara, Wil. *From Sharks to . . . Swimsuits*. Ann Arbor, MI: Cherry Lake Publishing, 2013.

NOTE TO EDUCATORS

Visit **www.focusreaders.com** to find lesson plans, activities, links, and other resources related to this title.

INDEX

Answer Key: 1. Answers will vary; **2.** Answers will vary; **3.** C; **4.** A